WILD
HORSES

WILD HORSES

Black Hills Sanctuary

by Cris Peterson

Photographs by Alvis Upitis

BOYDS MILLS PRESS

Author's Note

The Institute of Range and the American Mustang (IRAM) is a nonprofit organization founded in 1988 by Dayton O. Hyde. The Institute owns an eleven-thousand-acre wild horse sanctuary in the Black Hills of South Dakota. More information about IRAM can be found at **www.gwtc.net/~iram/**

Text copyright © 2003 by Cris Peterson
Photographs copyright © 2003 by Alvis Upitis
Boyds Mills Press, Inc.
A Highlights Company
815 Church Street
Honesdale, Pennsylvania 18431
Printed in China
Visit our Web site at www.boydsmillspress.com

Publisher Cataloging-in-Publication Data (U.S.)

Peterson, Cris.
Wild horses : Black Hills sanctuary / by Cris
Peterson ; photographs by Alvis Upitis. —1st ed.
[32] p. : col. photos. ; cm.
Summary: A view of life in the Black Hills Wild Horse Sanctuary and its efforts to save the American Mustang.
ISBN 1-56397-745-1
1. Wild horses—Black Hills (S.D.). 2. Mustang—Black Hills (S.D.).
I. Upitis, Alvis. II. Title
599.665/ 5/ 0978 21   2003
2002110799

First edition, 2003
Book design by Amy Drinker, Aster Designs
The text of this book is set in 16-point Adobe Garamond.
10 9 8 7 6 5 4 3 2 1

For Dayton Hyde

—C. P.

To Alise and Andris and their gentle strength

—Love, Dad

In the deepest, darkest part of night,

when the crickets and tree frogs are almost silent, shadowy shapes emerge from the ponderosa pine ridge and tiptoe down to the glassy Cheyenne River below. Their long tangled manes and tails ruffle in the night breeze. Ever alert and watchful for predators, they swiftly drink their fill. Then they turn on their heels and lunge up the rocky hills to safety.

In the misty glow of dawn, one can see these mysterious visitors aren't backyard pasture mares with swishing tails and docile, trusting eyes. These horses are wild—from another century, another era, another world. They are American mustangs, whose freedom, adaptability, and toughness define the western wilderness.

 Some of the mares have names. Medicine Hattie is easy to spot. Her dark ears jut out above her ghostly white face and corn-silk mane. Painted Lady's pure white coat is splashed with brown spots; she always seems to know where the sweetest grasses are.

 And there are others. Funny Face has a creamy white blaze that slides down the sides of her face like melting ice cream on a hot day. She loves to stand on the highest rock-strewn spot with her face to the wind. Yuskeya, whose name means freedom in the Sioux language, always stands at the edge of the herd, alert for danger and ready to run.

To find these horses, cross Cascade Creek where the South Dakota Black Hills meet the prairie, and turn right onto a pothole-strewn gravel road. This is the land of silver sagebrush and cowboy legends. Scraggly buzzards perch on fence posts near the entry gate to the Black Hills Wild Horse Sanctuary, home for more than three hundred wild horses and one determined cowboy-conservationist named Dayton Hyde.

Dayton was a gangly, growing thirteen-year-old boy when he met his first horse. It was a dirt-colored pony he found drinking from a puddle of old soapy dishwater behind his family's summer cabin in northern Michigan. He recalls that for a time he thought all horses blew bubbles out of their noses.

Soon after that encounter, word came from Dayton's cattle rancher uncle in Oregon that his cowboys had just captured a band of wild horses. Dayton hopped a westbound train and arrived on his uncle's doorstep, where he grew up as a cowboy learning to love the western range and its wild horses.

Mustangs are descendants of the horses brought to America by Spanish explorers nearly five hundred years ago. By 1900, more than two million smart, fast, surefooted wild horses roamed the West.

When newly invented barbed-wire fences began crisscrossing the rangelands, the horses lost access to sources of food and water and became a pesky problem for local residents. Thousands of them were slaughtered for fertilizer or pet food. By 1950, less than seventeen thousand survived.

After a Congressional act prohibited the capture or slaughter of wild horses in 1971, the wild horse population again grew quickly. Many died of thirst and starvation in the harsh western winters. In an attempt to manage the size of the herds, the United States government gathered up the animals and maintained them in fenced feedlots until they could be adopted.

One day in the early 1980s, Dayton Hyde, who by this time owned his uncle's ranch and had a grown family of his own, drove by one of these feedlots. Shocked and dismayed by the sight of dozens of muddy and dejected horses locked in a corral, he felt he had to do something.

After months of searching and many long days spent convincing government officials to accept his plan of creating a special place for wild horses, he acquired eleven thousand acres of rangeland and rimrock near the Black Hills in South Dakota. Here, among yawning canyons and sun-drenched pastures, he hoped wild horses—some too ugly, old, or knobby kneed to be adopted—could run free forever.

Before he could ship his wild horse rejects to their new home, Dayton had to build eight miles of fences to ensure they wouldn't wander into his neighbors' wheat fields. He also fenced in a fifty-acre training field where the horses would spend their first few days on the ranch adjusting to their new surroundings.

On a miserably cold fall day, huge creaking semi-trailers filled with snorting, stomping steeds finally arrived at the ranch. After hours of coaxing, Dayton succeeded in getting Magnificent Mary to skitter off the trailer. She was a battle-scarred, mean-eyed mare with a nose about twice as long as it should be. The rest of the herd clattered behind her, eyes bulging with fear.

Dayton's worst fear was that the horses would spook and charge through his carefully constructed six-wire fence, scattering across the prairie like dry leaves in a whirlwind. Aware that wild horses often feel threatened by being watched, he sat in the cab of his old pickup truck, peeking at them out of a corner of his eye. Finally, after nearly a week of around-the-clock vigilance, he swung open the gate from the training field to his wild horse sanctuary.

Many years have passed since Dayton held his breath and pushed that corral gate open. Every spring, dozens of his wild horses give birth to tottering colts that learn the ways of the back country from their mothers. They share the vast, quiet land with coyotes, mountain lions, and countless deer. Star lilies, bluebells, and prairie roses nod in the wind along with the prairie short grass that feeds the herd.

Thousands of visitors arrive each summer to get a glimpse of wild horses in their natural habitat, a habitat that has been preserved through Dayton's careful planning. Throughout the grazing season, he moves the herd from one area of the ranch to another so the horses don't damage the fragile rangeland. In the process, he searches for his marker mares: Painted Lady, Medicine Hattie, Funny Face, Yuskeya, Magnificent Mary, and several others. When he spots them all, he knows the whole herd is accounted for.

Sometimes in the fall while he's checking on the horses, Dayton notices a gaunt, aging mare whose ribs stand out through her ragged coat. He knows this old friend won't survive the winter. As the pale December daylight slips over the rimrock, the old mare lies down and goes to sleep for the last time. After years of running free, the wild mustang returns to the earth and completes the circle of life.

    The wild mustangs Dayton Hyde once discovered crowded into
a feedlot now gallop across the Cheyenne River free as the prairie wind.
They splash through the glistening water and bolt up a ravine. Here in
this rugged wilderness, one man's vision of a sanctuary for wild horses
has become a reality.